This Book Belongs To:

....

....

....

For Mollie & Daisy.

First published 2024 by Johnny Magory Business. Ballynafagh, Prosperous, Naas, Co. Kildare, Ireland.

ISBN: 978-1-7391437-3-2

www.JohnnyMagory.com
Edited by Aoife Barrett, Dublin
Printed by KPS Colour Print, Mayo

I'll tell you a story about two ponies I knew,
Named Mollie Maloney and Daisy Magoo.
Together they were happy, the perfect team,
Prancing in their paddock - every child's dream.

The friends met a long time ago on Lakeside Farm,
A retreat centre for ponies, full of country charm.
Mollie struck up a friendship, with Daisy the earth mother,
Polite and kind, they'd hold the paddock gates for each other.

You see, Daisy Magoo was known worldwide,
As a Zen-Master Guru and spiritual guide.

Her books were bestsellers, hot-topic news.
Her TedTalk on YouTube had

TEN MILLION VIEWS!

While Mollie Maloney was strong, fast and nimble,
Her show jumping rosettes were her status symbol.
She practised her jumping; Mollie just didn't rest,
But with all her training, she was still second best.

Mollie didn't like leaving Daisy for too long,
It made her feel sad; she just felt all wrong.
You see no matter how brave she tried to be,
Poor Mollie suffered terribly with anxiety.

Her stomach would knot, mean voices filled her head,
She'd fart, get the runs and then shake with dread!

Mollie was calmer when Daisy smiled and waited,
But one day the worst happened... they got SEPARATED!

They were out in their paddock on a wet winter's day,
When they decided to retreat to their stable for hay.

But how the rain fell and how the wind cried,
As Mollie followed Daisy back inside.

When suddenly a HURRICANE took Mollie away,
Miles from home on that fateful day.

Mollie panicked and farted; she got the runs bad,
She put her head in her hoofs, she was so sad.
She needed her Daisy, her comfort blanket for sure,

But then Mollie said "I must make it back home,
And I'll have to be very brave and do it alone."

Then she remembered
Daisy saying her

'INSTINCT'

was <u>always</u> right.

Mollie shut her eyes tightly and took a deep breath,
She felt a nudge inside tell her to go left.
But it led to water, one of her biggest fears,

But Daisy said to

'TRUST'

so Mollie wiped away her tears.

As she splashed through the water what did she see?
That her path was blocked by a HUGE fallen tree.

She panicked, she farted, her head filled with doom,

But Daisy said

'PERSPECTIVE'

helps new ideas bloom.

Mollie shut her eyes tightly and took a long, deep breath in,
And when she opened them, she saw a gap that made her grin,

She crawled under the oak tree, edging forward on her belly,
But when she stood up on the other side, her legs turned to jelly.

A swamp lay before her, with quicksand at the side,
A few stepping-stones marked the way like a guide.
Some logs floated by, but then she noticed one smile,
It wasn't a log - it was a snapping

CROCODILE!

She couldn't go back, and forward was frightful,

But Daisy had said that she should be

'MINDFUL'.

So Mollie took a deep breath,
in fact she took <u>three</u>,

And she crossed the stones with mindful glee.

She was proud of herself for getting that far,
She trotted on quickly then saw something bizarre.
From the corner of her eye, she heard a moan beside her,
With eight eyes and legs... it was a giant

SPIDER!

Mollie got such a fright she nearly jumped in the ditch,
The spider looked terrifying, and had an eight-legged twitch,

But Daisy had talked about the

'BEAUTY WITHIN',

So Mollie took a deep breath and tried a friendly grin.

"How do you do?" she asked the spider politely,
The spider smiled; she really wasn't that unsightly.
"I could do with a friend,"
the spider said sweetly.
"Me too,"
sighed Mollie, agreeing completely.

When the pair said goodbye, Mollie was nearly home,
And she was full of pride for how much she'd grown.

She'd learned about

INSTINCT,
PERSPECTIVE
AND TRUST,

About being

MINDFUL

and she had

INNER-BEAUTY

sussed.

And with a loud whiney, Daisy welcomed her friend,
Then resumed her meditation and yoga back bend,
"I knew you could do it," Daisy smiled, through wise eyes,

Mollie's next competition was the following day,
She wanted to be number one and go all the way.
"Goodbye Daisy," she said, and this time didn't shake,
She knew now there was no need to let her heart ache.

Using all the new tools she now knew were inside,
She levitated over the jumps, beaming with pride.
Her fans all went wild, screaming, "Go on Mollie Maloney!"
By the end of the day she was the

NUMBER ONE JUMPING PONY!

So that is the tale of two ponies I knew,
Called Mollie Maloney and Daisy Magoo,

Who no matter if they were together or apart,
Were the

GREATEST TWO PONIES

...even with the odd fart!

UNDERSTANDING OUR INNER STRENGTHS

INSTINCT

Instinct is like a little voice inside animals and people that tells them what to do without thinking about it. It's something they are born knowing how to do. For example, birds know how to build nests, and babies know how to cry when they need something. These are instincts, and they help living things survive and stay safe.

PERSPECTIVE

Perspective is like the way you see and understand things. Imagine you and a friend are looking at the same tree, but you see it from different sides. Your friend might see a bird's nest, and you might see a squirrel. Both views are correct, just different. Perspective is about seeing things from your own special spot, and understanding that others might see things differently from their spot.

TRUST

Trusting in yourself means believing that you can do things and make good choices. It's like having a little cheerleader inside you saying, "You can do it!" When you trust yourself, you feel confident trying new things, solving problems, and doing your best, even if it's hard. It's knowing that you are capable and strong.

MINDFUL

Being mindful means paying close attention to what you are doing right now. It's like turning on your super senses to notice everything around you, like how the air feels, what sounds you hear, and how your body feels. It also means noticing your thoughts and feelings without getting upset or distracted. Being mindful helps you stay calm and enjoy each moment.

INNER BEAUTY

Inner beauty is about the kind and good things inside a person. It means being nice, caring, and helpful to others. When someone has inner beauty, they are friendly, honest, and make people feel happy and loved. It's what makes a person truly special, more than just how they look on the outside.

<u>About the Author</u>

Emma-Jane Leeson is a best-selling author, yoga teacher and writing coach from county Kildare, Ireland.

This book was inspired by her two ponies Mollie and Daisy who live with her and her children, their donkey Richard, goat brothers Patrick & Sean, dogs Freddie & Peter and cats Whiskers, TomToo, Garfield & Ronnie.

The photography in this book is by Emma-Jane and shows some of her favourite places in Ireland and some of her four-legged furry family! Emma-Jane is passionate about nature and empowering children to be, do, have and pursue everything they want to. She hopes she can make a small difference through her books and yoga.

...She's also pony mad!

P.S - Can you spot her hiding on one of the pages?

Visit www.JohnnyMagory.com to learn more about her other books.